Pioneer Cat

By William H. Hooks
Illustrated by Charles Robinson

A STEPPING STONE BOOK

Random House New York

Library of Congress Cataloging-in-Publication Data:
Hooks, William H. Pioneer cat / by William H. Hooks ; illustrated by Charles Robinson. p. cm.—(A Stepping stone book) SUMMARY: When a young pioneer girl smuggles a cat aboard the wagon train taking her family from Missouri to Oregon, it turns out to be the best thing she could have done. ISBN: 0-394-82038-X (pbk.); 0-394-92038-4 (lib. bdg.) [1. Cats—Fiction. 2. Overland journeys to the Pacific—Fiction. 3. Oregon Trail—Fiction. 4. Frontier and pioneer life—Fiction.] I. Robinson, Charles, ill. II. Title. PZ7.H7664Pi 1988 [E]—dc 19 88-4708

Manufactured in the United States of America   23 22 21 20 19 18 17 16 15 14

Contents

1
Snuggs

For two days I rode in the back of the dusty wagon and cried. I was one big mess. Feeling sorry for myself. And mad at my whole family.

Pa stopped the wagon. Everybody got out to eat. Everybody but me. I just sat where I was, moping instead of crying. I'd run dry on tears.

"Kate Purdy, are you going to eat something?" asked my ma.

"You know I can't swallow when I'm upset," I told Ma.

"Leave her be," said Pa. "My Katie has a mind and a stomach of her own."

"I'll take her gingerbread," said Duffy. He's my brother. He's one year older, but not a bit smarter than me. Duffy can eat anything, anytime. Upset or not.

Ma plunked Benjy into my lap. "Well, if you're not going to eat, how about looking after your baby brother?"

Benjy's a cute little rascal. But it seemed to me that Ma could just once in a while ask Duffy to look after him. I was busy thinking about Doris. And our nice house in Jackson, Mississippi. And how perfect everything was back there.

We stayed in Jackson two whole years. That's the longest we were ever in one place. And the only place I had had a real friend. When I was little I had wanted a sister. Doris was better than a sister. I might have been jealous of a real sister. Not so with Doris. Just like Ma said, we were "two peas from the same pod."

We swore to be friends forever, me and Doris. But that creaky old wagon was putting more miles between us every day.

Benjy and Duffy liked traveling in the wagon, the same as Pa. Ma's not the complaining sort. She just takes her lot as it comes, with a smile. Me, I hated it.

Ma's said to me many a time, "Your Pa's got itchy feet. He's a traveling man. He'll keep moving west till we run out of land, I reckon."

Well, I reckon that's why we left Jackson—the perfect place as far as I was concerned. Duffy was all excited about going to Saint Joseph, Missouri.

"Saint Joe! The jumping-off place for the wild unknown!" Duffy shouted over and over till I was sick of it.

It was where Pa was bringing us to join a wagon train headed for Oregon.

It took us two weeks to reach Saint Joe. By the time we rolled into town I was sick of *me.* Sometimes you can get so tired of feeling sorry for yourself you just quit. Sort of like you've used up all your worry power.

When we got to Saint Joe it was Pa and Duffy's turn to be disappointed. We were too late for the wagon train. It had been gone a week. We'd have to wait a month for the next one.

After our long, miserable ride from Jackson things moved pretty fast. By late afternoon we were set up in two little rooms on Mudd Street.

And Pa had himself a job with the New West Harness Company.

Me and Ma set to straightening up things. Pa and Duffy went off to look around Saint Joe. I was feeling put out that I didn't get to go.

"Boys have all the fun," I said to Benjy. "You don't know how lucky you are."

It was night by the time Pa and Duffy came back. Me and Ma had supper ready. We all crowded around the table and joined hands. Pa said grace and we all said, "Amen." Benjy kept clapping his hands and saying, "Men, men, men!"

After supper Ma spread two pallets on the kitchen floor for me and Duffy. Pa and Ma and Benjy took the big bed in the other room.

I think I was sound asleep before I got the covers over me.

At first I thought I was dreaming. I kept hearing a sound. A sad little crying sound. I sat up and listened in the dark. "Meow, meow," came the cry. Right outside the door.

I pushed the quilt away and tiptoed to the

door. I didn't want to wake Duffy. As quietly as I could, I opened the door. A bright patch of moonlight shot into the room. I peeked through the crack. There was a little silver-gray cat.

"Meow, meow," cried the thin little cat.

"Sh, sh!" I whispered. "You'll wake everybody up."

The little cat seemed to understand. It stopped meowing and squeezed in the door.

"Hey, hold on," I whispered. "Ma don't hold with cats in the house."

But I didn't want to put the little cat out. So I closed the door and scooted back to my pallet. Soon I could feel the cat moving close to me. She nosed into the pallet and settled down against my arm.

"You like snuggling up, don't you, little cat?" I whispered. "I think I'll call you Snuggs."

2

Secrets

Before dawn I woke up. For a minute I thought the whole thing had been a dream. But there was the cat snuggled up under my quilt.

I crept onto the porch and put her out. "Stay under the porch and keep quiet," I said.

I sneaked back in the house and crumbled some corn bread in a saucer of milk. Then I took it to Snuggs under the porch.

When Ma came out to the yard later that morning, Snuggs ran up to her.

"Kate," Ma called, "there's a little half-starved cat out here."

I tried not to sound too interested. "I saw her already," I said.

"We ought to give her something to eat," said Ma.

"You mean we can let her stay?" I asked cautiously.

"It's fine by me," said Ma. "Just as long as she keeps her place in the yard."

Her place at night is under my quilt, I thought. But all I said was, "Thank you, Ma."

Pa worked all day at the New West Harness Company. One night I baked him an apple pie. It's one of the things I can cook right. Pa said to me, "I'm glad to see my Katie's getting back some of her spit-and-vinegar. There's a rosy future for anybody who can bake like this."

It made me feel good. But I was holding back on Pa for yanking us up and dragging us off to Saint Joe. Leaving my best friend was still a sore point.

"Missing that wagon train may turn out to be a blessing," said Pa.

"Why?" asked Ma.

"It'll give me time to bargain for all the things we'll need for Oregon," answered Pa.

First Pa bought extra horses. Then he traded our old wagon in on a big new one with a canvas top.

"How does she look?" he cried.

"Looks like a cross between a boat and a wagon," said Ma.

"That's why they call these contraptions prairie schooners," said Pa.

"We're going to sail her all the way to Oregon!" shouted Duffy.

I had to laugh. The wagon did look like a ship, with its big white canvas top. Then I felt that old choking thing in my throat again. What a lot of fun it would be, traveling in the prairie schooner, if only Doris could come along.

Our small rooms were crammed with things for the trip. Duffy and I hardly had space for our pallets. Bags of dried beans, tin buckets of lard and brown sugar, and jars of apple jelly crowded around our beds. When I looked up at night, I was staring at slabs of bacon and dried beef hanging from the ceiling.

"We'll need food enough to last us through six months," said Ma.

Saint Joe was filling up fast. New wagons pulled in, crammed with goods and people. New children and dogs were all over the place.

Ma said, "I'll bet you'll make lots of new friends in the wagon train."

"No thanks," I told her. "I was perfectly happy with my old friends."

Ma gave me that look I get when I know I'm trying her patience. To tell the truth, I was using most of my worry power on what to do about Snuggs. Not much was left over for Doris. I was afraid to even ask if I could take a stray cat on the trip. I already knew the answer.

My worry came to a head the day Pa said, "Time to pack the wagon. Captain Jonah, the trail boss, says the train moves out tomorrow."

Pa and Duffy loaded all the heavy boxes into the wagon.

I was half sick with worry. My brain just felt dazed. I couldn't come up with one single way to take Snuggs along.

That night Ma gave Duffy and me each a small box.

"It's going to be hard to fit everything in the wagon," she said. "But all of us ought to have our own little space. You can take anything you want, as long as it fits into your box."

I took my box out on the porch. It wouldn't hold much. Maybe my doll with the china head. And the hair ribbons Doris had given me. Suddenly Snuggs brushed against my leg. I patted her head and started talking to her.

"I've just got to think of a way to take you with me. You're as good a friend as I ever had.

And I'm not going to leave you. You can count on that."

Snuggs jumped into my lap. She landed right in the box. My worry-sick brain finally snapped into action.

"That's it, Snuggs!" I cried. "You've solved our problem. Ma said I could take anything on the trip as long as it fit in my box. And you just fit!"

I punched holes in the box while I explained things to Snuggs.

"These are air holes for you. You've got to stay still. No noise until we're far out on the prairie. Understand?"

Snuggs swished her tail and tried to put her paw through one of the holes. I think she did understand.

I was so tired that night, I couldn't fall asleep. I kept whispering to Snuggs, "Tomorrow's the day. Tomorrow's the day."

Finally I slept and dreamed.

Doris and I were riding on the front seat of the wagon. Snuggs was sitting in my lap. Captain Jonah rode up on his snow-white horse. "That's a mighty fine-looking cat you young ladies have there," he said. "Pity your folks didn't tell you we don't allow cats on the trail. They're bad luck. You'll have to get rid of it. Sorry, Miss."

I woke up really scared. "Doris," I called. Then I saw all the stuff around me for the wagon train and knew where I was. I felt for Snuggs under the quilt. She was gone!

3
Wagons, Ho!

I was stuffing my feet into my shoes to go looking for Snuggs. I heard the door to Ma's room open.

"Kate," called Ma. "See after Benjy while I get breakfast."

I took Benjy outside to look for Snuggs. I couldn't find her anywhere. I was panicky and mad, too. Of all the days to go wandering off, this was the worst one. Leaving Saint Joe was going to be just as bad as leaving Jackson.

At breakfast Pa said grace. "Dear Lord, give us a good journey and safekeeping. And bring us finally to Oregon if it be thy will."

I added my own silent plea, "And please include Snuggs."

We rolled up our bedding and put it in the wagon. I helped Ma hang her pots on big hooks on the outside of the wagon. Still no sign of Snuggs. I was so worried, I was afraid I might cry. Then I'd have Ma asking me what was the matter.

Pa said, "I'm going to drive the wagon to the front of the house. Just to see how she pulls." We all watched.

Duffy bounced up beside Pa.

"Giddup!" shouted Pa.

The horses strained under the load. The wagon jerked forward. That's when I saw something shoot out of the back of the wagon.

It was Snuggs! She had been hiding in the wagon. She scooted into the house. I was sure no one else saw her.

"She rides real smooth," called Pa. "Everybody hop in."

Ma climbed up with Benjy.

"Where's Kate?" asked Pa.

"Kate!" yelled Ma.

"I forgot my box," I called from inside.

I opened the box and tapped the side, "Here Snuggs!" She hopped in, and I closed the lid.

"Don't you make a sound. Don't you even purr," I warned.

"Kate!" Ma called.

I ran out and climbed into the back of the wagon, clutching my box.

The grove outside Saint Joe where the wagon train formed looked like a big campground. Children ran yelling and playing around the wagons. Dogs joined in, barking and chasing after the kids.

Pa finally found Captain Jonah. He gave Pa a number for our wagon—number 49.

Duffy asked Pa if he could carve our number on the side of the wagon.

"You can do more than that," said Pa. "We've got to keep track of the days. Carve a notch for each weekday and a long mark for each Sunday."

I felt cheated. Pa always gave Duffy the important things to do.

But Pa surprised me. "Come with me, Katie girl," he said. "I've got a special job for you."

Pa lifted up a round tin can from under the

wagon seat. Then he showed me how to put axle grease on the big wagon wheels.

"Every day before it gets dark I want you to grease each wheel, Kate. Then check all the spokes for cracks. Let me know if you find anything wrong."

I stared at the big wheels. They were as tall as me.

Pa said, "It's wheels that will get us to

Oregon. You've got a sharp eye, Katie. I'm trusting our wheels to you."

Pa managed to get our wagon through all the confusion. Finally we found wagon number 48. We pulled up behind it.

Toward the front of the line we could hear a lot of shouting.

"I can't make it out," said Pa.

At first I couldn't make it out either. Then I got it clear. "They're shouting, 'Wagons, ho!' " I cried.

Duffy was the first to join in. "Wagons, ho!" he hollered.

The air was ringing with "Wagons, ho!" It was exciting, I had to admit. Before I knew it, I was yelling, "Wagons, ho!" too.

The white tops of the wagons in front of us started bobbing up and down.

"Giddup!" shouted Pa.

"Oregon, here we come!" yelled Duffy.

I crawled over the boxes and sacks to the back of the wagon. I raised the lid of my box. Snuggs opened a sleepy eye and yawned at me.

"We're on our way, Miss Snuggs," I whispered. "So far, so good."

4
Night on the Prairie

The canvas-topped wagons were like ovens. Duffy and I found we could walk as fast as the train moved. It was a lot cooler to walk, too.

I worried about Snuggs. How long could she stay cooped up?

The first day we were walking beside the wagon, I met a big girl who was in wagon 48. She was a sight. Wild, curly, carrot-colored hair shot out in all directions around her head. Her calico dress looked about two sizes too large. She wore it hitched up so you could see the big brogan shoes on her feet.

This big carrot-headed girl walked right up to me and said, "My name's Rosie Murphy. What's yours?"

"Kate Purdy," I told her.

"Let's be best friends," said Rosie.

Before I could tell her I already had a best friend, she said, "Now that's settled. You can count on me to look after you!"

"But I don't need anybody to look after me," I told her.

"Beans!" she said. "Everybody needs a friend, Kate Purdy. I'm the best looker-after you'll ever meet. I do all the looking-after for my pa."

"What about your ma?" I asked.

"Ma's dead a year now," she said.

"And you cook and wash and do everything?" I asked.

"Everything," boomed Rosie. "I promised Ma I'd look after Pa."

We walked along for a few minutes without talking. I noticed one thing about Rosie that was really nice. She had green sparkly eyes that looked like they were smiling.

Then Rosie said, "Stick with me, honey. You won't have a thing to worry about. Let's shake on it."

She stuck out her hand. But I just stood there like a dummy. I couldn't do it. It would be like betraying Doris.

• • •

When the shadows started getting long, a message came down the line of wagons. "Campsite for the night. About a mile ahead!"

My worries about Snuggs flared up again. How could I get her out of the box without being seen? How could I sneak food to her? What would Ma and Pa do if they found out?

By the time we made the circle with the wagons it was late afternoon. Pa and Duffy unhitched the horses to let them graze on grass. I helped Ma get a cook fire started. Then I got the tin bucket from under the wagon seat and greased the wheels. I felt every spoke. They were smooth as glass.

When I put the bucket back in the wagon seat, I saw my chance to let Snuggs out for a minute. No one was in the wagon but Benjy. And he was asleep.

I opened the box lid. Snuggs hopped out and jumped from the wagon. My heart thumped. What if somebody saw her? I figured I'd have to take the chance. The poor cat had been penned up all day.

I waited in the wagon about a minute. Then

I peeked out. There was Snuggs covering a small hole under the wagon.

"Good girl," I whispered. I tapped my fingers against the side of the wagon. Snuggs jumped back in.

"Kate!" called Ma.

I caught my breath. Ma saw her, I thought. But she called again, "Kate! Bring me the frying pan."

I stuffed Snuggs back in the box and rushed out to Ma with the pan.

Supper on the prairie that first night was delicious. Cook fires circled the big camp. There was lots of visiting back and forth.

Rosie came barreling over to our campfire. She didn't give me a chance to even introduce her.

"I'm Rosie Murphy," she said, grabbing first Ma's, then Pa's, hand. When she went for Duffy, he stepped back and just nodded his head.

"Welcome," said Ma. "Would you like some coffee?"

"No, I'm full as a boardinghouse bedbug," said Rosie, patting her stomach.

Everyone laughed. Then Rosie settled down

with us like a longtime friend. In one of the wagons someone was playing a fiddle. I looked up at the sky. About a million sparkling stars were winking at me. It was a perfect night. Except for two things. With all these people around, I was lonely. I wondered what Doris was doing right then. And I knew Snuggs must be very hungry.

When the fire burned low, Rosie said, "I'd better be getting back before my pa sends out the scouts."

Pa yawned and said, "Let's all get to bed. Tomorrow we'll drive all day."

Rosie said, "Kate, how about walking me over to wagon number 48?"

On the way over I got an idea about Snuggs. I asked Rosie, "Did you mean what you said?"

"I said about a million things. Which one?" asked Rosie.

"About looking after somebody, if they needed it."

"You need some looking-after already?" asked Rosie.

"Well, it's for a friend of mine," I said.

Then I told Rosie about Snuggs.

"That's a bunch of tough beans you got there," she said. "I can't believe you thought you could hide a cat all the way to Oregon."

"Well, not all the way," I said. "But far enough so my folks will let me keep her."

"I can see it coming." Rosie laughed, and said, "You want me to take your cat in our wagon. Right?"

And that was how I made a deal with Rosie. When the family was asleep, she came to our wagon. I told her I wanted to pay her for keeping Snuggs, but she didn't want to take anything for it. I made her take one of my hair ribbons for pay, anyway. I figured her hair could surely use one.

5
Buffalo

From the first day, Duffy was asking, "When are we going to see some buffalo?"

But he had carved ten notches on the wagon before we spotted any.

"I'd sure like to see one of them beasts up close!" he cried.

"I like them right where they are," I said.

In a way I soon got a lot closer to the buffalo. We ran out of firewood and had to burn dried buffalo droppings. They were called "chips."

Ma didn't fancy picking them up.

Rosie didn't seem to mind a bit.

"Come on, Kate," she called. "We'll collect enough for me and your ma."

• • •

The longer we were on the trail, the hotter it got. Everybody was glad to see the sun set. At least it was cooler at night. But when night came, so did thousands of buffalo gnats. The only way to keep from being eaten alive was to sit close to the campfires. The gnats hated smoke more than they liked humans. When I sneaked over to Rosie's wagon to see Snuggs, I got dozens of bites.

Late one afternoon Rosie and I were counting the notches Duffy had carved.

"It's hard to believe we've been on the trail almost three weeks," I said.

"Not for me," said Rosie. "I feel like I've already walked three thousand miles. And picked up a million buffalo chips!"

While we were laughing, I heard a rumbling sound. "You hear that?" I asked.

"Sounds like thunder," said Rosie.

From the front of the train two scouts came riding toward us.

"Swing the wagons in a circle!" they shouted.

"What's wrong?" asked Pa.

"Buffalo stampede!" shouted the scouts.

The rumbling was growing louder.

Rosie ran to her wagon.

In a few minutes the wagons were in a ragged circle. Ma and I ducked under the wagon with Benjy. Pa and Duffy grabbed guns and crawled behind the big wagon wheels.

All I could see was a big dark cloud moving toward us.

"Where are the buffalo?" I asked.

"In that dust cloud," said Pa. "There must be thousands of them."

Captain Jonah rode up. "Have your guns ready!" he shouted. "But don't shoot until I give you the word."

The buffalo were close. I could taste dust in my mouth. Then, in the moving dust cloud, I saw them. They were packed tight, like a solid wall. Their heads were down. Their tails were in the air. The ground shook under their pounding hooves.

"Hold your fire!" commanded Captain Jonah.

I was sure they'd crush us any second. I closed my eyes.

"Fire! Fire! Fire!" shouted Captain Jonah.

The guns barked and my eyes flew open.

Several buffalo in the front of the pack crumpled to the ground. More piled up behind them. But one huge wounded beast kept coming. He plowed into a wagon near ours. There was this sickening thud. The wagon rolled over.

I heard screams. And more gunfire. The huge shaggy buffalo was slumped against a schooner. A red stain was spreading in the sand around the dead buffalo. I felt sick.

But the gunfire was working. The solid line of buffalo split in the middle. They turned away from the pile of dead buffalo and ran past the wagons. I could see hundreds of brown shaggy legs flying by our wagon.

"We've broken the stampede!" shouted Captain Jonah.

The mad, rushing buffalo swung wide of the wagons. Soon the last of the huge herd passed us by. The dust began to settle. The thundering roar of the stampede faded away.

"We're safe now," said Pa. "I'm going over to help the folks in the overturned wagon."

I crawled from under the wagon and shook the dust off. Then I ran over to Rosie's wagon to check on Snuggs. The lid was off the little box. It was empty. Snuggs was gone.

6
Out of the Box

I looked everywhere in the wagon for Snuggs. I called and called. She just wasn't there. I was still shaking from the buffalo. It was too much for me. First Doris. And now Snuggs. Everything I loved got taken away. I started crying.

Rosie came panting up. "You can swap them tears for a smile," she cried. "Not a scratch on a living soul. And only one busted wagon."

"Snuggs is gone!" I blurted out. "And it's all your fault."

Rosie just ignored my saying it was her fault. "Did you check out the wagon?" she asked.

"Every inch. And I called and called."

"Maybe she went back to your wagon. Hurry! Now's the best time to search. Everybody's over at the wrecked schooner."

But there was no trace of Snuggs in our wagon.

Ma came back with Benjy and caught me still crying.

"It's all right, Kate," said Ma. "They're gone. Everyone is safe."

I wanted to tell Ma about Snuggs. But I didn't dare. I wiped my eyes and went with Rosie back to her wagon.

"I got some scouting to do," said Rosie. "Get back to your wagon and keep calm."

Back at the wagon Pa told us we were going to stay put for the night. "It'll give us time to skin some buffalo for supper," he said.

"And maybe time to find Snuggs," I said to myself.

Duffy went with Pa to skin the dead buffalo.

I started greasing the wagon wheels. Terrible pictures of little Snuggs trampled by the buffalo kept racing through my mind.

The men came back with big buffalo steaks. Ma fixed some for our supper. I couldn't eat the tough meat. I just sat there, hoping Rosie would turn up.

"You're mighty quiet, Katie," said Pa.

"The buffalo gave her a bad scare," said Ma.

I kept quiet and let them think that's what was bothering me.

Me and Ma cleaned up after supper. Still no Rosie. And she didn't show up by the time we all went to bed.

It was a terrible night for me. I couldn't sleep. Finally I gave up and crept to the back of the wagon.

"Snuggs, Snuggs," I called quietly. But there was no answer.

I stared out across the starlit prairie. It felt so lonely. As far as I could see there was nothing—just flat prairie stretching on and on.

"Kate!" someone called softly.

I was so frightened I almost fell out of the wagon.

"I found her!" cried Rosie, rushing up in her long white nightgown.

She had Snuggs under her arm.

"Snuggs! Snuggs!" I cried. I was grateful to Rosie. "Where was she?" I asked.

"Who knows?" said Rosie. "I woke up, and there she was, snuggled up to me like a bedbug in a new mattress."

We made so much noise it woke up the whole family.

"What's going on?" asked Ma. She couldn't believe what she saw in my arms.

Pa called, "What's all this racket about?"

"That little stray cat Kate befriended in Saint Joe has followed us all these miles!" cried Ma.

Rosie looked at me and winked.

But I didn't wink back. I knew I had to tell them the truth.

"Ma, Snuggs didn't find us," I said. "I brought her with me."

"But, I don't understand," said Ma.

"Remember you said I could bring anything that would fit in my box?"

"Well, yes," answered Ma. "But I never dreamed . . ."

I explained the whole thing.

"Well, that's a humdinger!" cried Pa.

"She can stay, can't she?" I asked.

"A deal's a deal," said Ma. "I couldn't go back on my word, could I?"

"No, ma'am," said Pa.

• • •

In the days that followed, children from all up and down the wagon train found their way to our wagon.

"Can I see the cat?" "Can I pet her?" "Does she eat buffalo meat?" they asked.

"If a cat could be spoiled rotten, this one would stink!" said Rosie.

For a change, I was having a good time on the trail. Then one afternoon Captain Jonah rode up while I had Snuggs in my lap. I remembered my bad dream about the captain, and cats not being allowed in the wagon train. I quickly flipped my apron over Snuggs. I hoped the captain hadn't seen her.

"Where's your pa?" he asked.

"Over there," I gasped, pointing in the opposite direction.

The captain rode away. I hid Snuggs in the wagon.

When Pa came back to our wagon, he said we would make camp early.

"Why?" asked Ma.

"Indians," said Pa. "They've been tracking us all day."

7

Indians

For three days the scouts reported: "Indians still tracking us."

"They probably only want to do some trading," Captain Jonah reassured us. "The important thing is that no one panics and does something foolish. I've brought many wagon trains through Indian country. Never had any real trouble."

It was late in the afternoon on the fourth day when I saw them.

At first they were tiny specks bobbing up and down far out on the plains.

"They're on horseback," said Rosie.

The scouts rushed up shouting, "Circle the wagons!"

As soon as the circle was made, Pa grabbed

his gun. Then he joined the men lined up behind Captain Jonah.

I peeked through a slit in the canvas. A long
line of Indians on horseback was moving slowly
toward us. It was so still and quiet, I could
hear everyone breathing in the wagon. Suddenly the Indians stopped.

Captain Jonah made a sign with his hands.

An Indian who must have been the chief re-
turned Captain Jonah's sign.

Then Captain Jonah and the chief rode out
and met in the middle.

For a few minutes they talked, and made
signs with their hands. Then Captain Jonah
turned and went back to his men. The chief
did the same.

Crack! A single gunshot rang out from one
of our wagons.

The pony one of the young Indians was riding stumbled and crashed to the ground. The
rider went down with him.

Our scouts raced back toward the wagon
train, yelling, "Hold your fire!"

The Indians pulled up around the wounded
pony and the fallen rider. Captain Jonah dashed

up to them and jumped off his horse. I was sure the Indians would kill him. Why didn't the scouts go to his rescue?

Instead the scouts kept yelling, "For God's sake, don't shoot!"

In a few minutes that seemed to last forever, the crowd around the fallen rider parted. The young Indian who had gone down with the pony looked dead.

The captain rushed back to the wagons. The Indians made a long line facing us. They just stood there, silent and threatening.

"Who fired that shot?" demanded the captain angrily.

Two scouts dragged a man from wagon 42.

"That was a stupid thing to do, Ned Bassett!" shouted the captain.

Ned started to protest. But Captain Jonah shouted, "I don't care about your excuses. I only care about the safety of the folks on this wagon train. I could hang you for disobeying orders. Or I could just hand you over to the Indians."

Ned's wife rushed up to Captain Jonah. She started pleading with him.

Captain Jonah motioned her away.

"All they wanted was to trade hides for blankets and sugar. Now the stakes are higher. Thank God the boy's only stunned. But the pony is dead. Either we supply them with four horses and sugar and blankets, or we can expect an attack. Those are the terms!"

The men started shouting all at once.

Captain Jonah held up his hand for silence.

"They're going to sit there for a half hour. If we don't have the horses and other stuff outside the wagon train by then, they're going to come swooping down on us. I've told the chief we'd meet their demands."

"How are we going to do that?" asked one of the men.

"Ned Bassett, you have four horses. Unhitch two of them for the Indians," commanded the captain.

"But only two horses can't pull my wagon," Ned protested.

"You can lighten your load by dumping some of it right here."

"Where are the other two horses coming from?" asked Pa.

"We'll take two from the extra horses my scouts carry," said the captain.

He motioned one of the scouts to bring the horses.

"Every wagon must give a pound of sugar and a blanket," said Captain Jonah. "And be quick about it! Our time is running out."

In just a few minutes we piled up a great mound of blankets and sugar. Captain Jonah and the scouts brought out the four horses. They staked them by the sugar and blankets. Then everyone pulled back behind the wagons.

"Keep your guns ready, men. But don't make

a move unless I give the order!" shouted Captain Jonah.

Suddenly the still, silent line of Indians exploded. They came racing toward us. They were yelling and waving guns and spears, kicking up clouds of dust. I expected arrows and bullets to rip through the wagon any second.

When they reached the staked horses and the pile of blankets and sugar, the Indians stopped in a cloud of dust.

I couldn't believe my eyes when I saw Snuggs gingerly sniffing her way over toward the pile of goods. Without thinking, I jumped from the wagon and raced after her. She was almost halfway to the Indians when I caught her. I scooped her up and rolled her in my apron. In the confusion no one noticed me until I was almost back.

"Get that child into a wagon!" Captain Jonah roared.

Pa dashed over and snatched me up so hard, it felt like he threw me back into the wagon. "That was dumb, Katie!" he shouted. "What came over you?"

"Snuggs—Snuggs—I was going after Snuggs,"

I stammered. I unrolled my apron to show I wasn't crazy. Snuggs hopped out.

"You put us through such a scare," said Ma.

I looked back. The Indians were dividing up the blankets and sugar. They were chattering and laughing and didn't seem the least bit warlike.

"Thank the Lord," said Pa.

Captain Jonah rode out to them and gave the chief a fine leather saddle.

Rosie called, "Hey, Kate, Indians are better than buffalo any day, huh?"

In less than an hour the Indians left. We watched until they were just tiny specks far out on the prairie. Then they vanished, and night came on.

That night as we sat around the campfire, Snuggs jumped into Rosie's lap. Rosie petted her. Then she got a puzzled look on her face.

"Kate, come over here!" she called.

"What is it?" I asked.

Rosie stood up. "Folks, I've got an announcement to make," she said. "We're going to have kittens before we reach Oregon!"

8
River Crossing

Captain Jonah pushed the wagon train hard after the Indian scare.

"This is the hard part of the trip," he said. "We've got a tough river to ford before we cross the mountains."

"But our horses are worn out," one of the men protested.

"Get out of the wagons and walk!" snapped the captain. Then he made it an order. "Everybody walks from here on."

All of us plodded along beside our wagons in the broiling sun.

"If you had three wishes, what would you wish for?" Rosie asked me.

"Ice, ice, and more ice!"

"Your wishes wouldn't last a minute in this heat," said Rosie. "If I had three wishes, I'd change into a cat and ride like Snuggs. Then I'd wave my tail like a wand and land us all in Oregon."

"What about your third wish?" I asked.

"Oh, once we got to Oregon I'd meet up with some nice tomcat. Then I'd use my third wish to change him into a prince, and me into Cinderella. And we'd have ice-cold lemonade every day!"

We kept walking for a whole week in the terrible heat.

One day we came upon a long line of boxes, trunks, and furniture scattered beside the trail. Rose and I ran over to see what was in the trunks.

"Keep moving!" shouted one of the scouts. "Just count yourself lucky we don't have to dump all our goods. Take a look over there!"

I gasped. Sun-bleached skeletons of horses lay in the sand.

"Their teams gave out," explained the scout. "They doubled up and went on as best they could. Move along now. We've got a river to ford up ahead."

By the time we reached the river, the scouts were struggling to get ropes strung across. The muddy water looked ready to overflow the riverbanks. The horses had a hard time making it across. But finally the scouts got two short ropes anchored across the river. Then the captain gave the signal.

"One driver to a wagon. Everybody else, over on the ropes!" he ordered.

The families ahead of us plunged into the water. They began pulling themselves along on the ropes. I tied Benjy on Ma's back.

Benjy cried, "Kitty, kitty!" and pointed to our wagon.

"Snuggs is all right," I told him. But he kept saying, "Kitty, kitty."

Pa drove our big schooner into the river.

"She floats like a boat!" he called.

We plunged into the water. I could see Rosie up ahead on the rope.

At first it felt good just to be cool again. Then in the deeper water I began to feel the strong pull of the undertow.

Duffy called from behind me. "Hey, this is fun!"

I was about to tell him to hold tight, since he'd soon be in the undertow. But Duffy shouted again. "Look, no hands!"

I turned. There he was, treading water with both hands off the rope.

"Duffy!" I called. "Stop that! You know you can't really swim!"

He struck the undertow and went under like a rock.

I was so scared, I couldn't even call for help. Duffy popped back up right next to me. He was coughing and spitting water. I grabbed his arm. But he was thrashing around so wildly, I lost my grip on the rope. We both went whirling toward the center of the river.

We shot right past Ma and Benjy. Ma screamed. I was sure we were lost. I still held on to Duffy, but his head kept bobbing under.

Then I hit something. Something hard that sent pain shooting up my arm. It was Rosie's wagon. I grabbed it. Then I pulled Duffy up close, where I could keep his head above water. He coughed, and spit more muddy water.

"Grab the wagon!" I yelled. He clawed at the side of the wagon and found a pot hook to hang on to. I was afraid to let him go. But my arm was hurting so, I didn't know how long I could hold on.

Suddenly Rosie was there with her arms around both Duffy and me. She had us penned against the wagon.

"Hang on!" she cried. "You all right, Duffy?"

He spit more water and mumbled, "I'm fine."

"You don't look too bad for someone who's just drunk half a river," said Rosie. "How about you, Kate?"

I was scared to death, and my arm was hurting something fierce. But I had to laugh at Rosie's saying Duffy didn't look so bad. "Now I'm fine too," I said.

Rosie clung to the wagon with us until we were across the river. Everyone cheered as we staggered up the muddy riverbank to safety. The three of us flopped on the ground and sat there, completely worn out.

I started to speak. But Rosie broke in. "Don't say anything right now."

I nodded.

Rosie held out her hand and asked, "Friends?"

I took Rosie's hand and nodded. "Yes." I was glad Rosie had ordered me not to speak. I was too choked up to say anything.

Just then Pa drove our wagon up the riverbank. And Ma staggered, wet and muddy, right
behind the wagon.

"Kate! Duffy!" she cried. "You're all right.
Thank God, you're all right!"

"We're fine," I said. "Except for my arm. It
hurts something awful."

Ma said, "Here Duffy, watch Benjy."

Benjy kept saying, "Kitty, kitty," like a par-
rot.

"Come into the wagon, Kate," said Ma. "I
want to check that arm."

Rosie helped me into the back of the wagon.
I glanced at Snugg's small box. It was empty.
Then I heard a faint squeaky sound. I looked
toward my pallet. There was Snuggs, washing
four tiny kittens.

"Well, what do you know?" I said to Rosie.
"I reckon this is what Benjy was trying to tell
me all along."

9
Oregon

By the time the kittens' eyes were open we had reached the mountains.

"Oregon's on the other side," announced Captain Jonah. "We've got a hard ride up, but an easy ride down. Let's start climbing!"

We all still had to walk. And when the trail got steeper, we had to help push the heavy wagons. But the cool in the mountains felt good.

The rocky trail was hard on wheels. Every day a wagon would have to pull out of line to fix a broken wheel. I still took care of our wheels. Even though my arm was hurt, I wouldn't let Duffy take over. I was superstitious about them. When the last one was checked, I'd pat it and say, "Lucky wheels! You'll get us there!"

Well, the luck played out before we reached the crest of the mountains. The whole family plus Rosie was pushing our wagon up a steep part of the trail. *Crack!* Our left front wheel hit a big rock.

"Knocked the iron rim completely off!" cried Pa. "We'll have to drop out of line and fix it."

"How long will it take?" I asked Pa.

"Maybe a half day," he answered.

Rosie helped us push the wagon aside to let the ones behind us pass. Then she ran ahead to her own wagon.

Captain Jonah rode up.

"Tough luck, Purdy," he said. "We're less than a day away from the crest. Then it's easy going. Tell you what we'll do. I'll camp an hour early tonight and start out an hour later tomorrow. That'll give you time to catch up."

Pa thanked the captain.

At that very moment, Benjy held up a kitten in the back of the wagon. "Kitty, kitty!" he cried.

Captain Jonah turned.

I caught the surprised look on his face. My old nightmare about the captain, and cats being bad luck on a wagon train, rushed back.

"Where in tarnation did that kitten come from?" roared the captain.

Benjy picked up another kitten. And another, and another.

"Kitty, kitty!" he kept saying, grinning at the captain.

Then Snuggs poked her head out of the back of the wagon.

"My God, what's this? A wagonload of cats!" exclaimed Captain Jonah.

I caught my breath and ran to the wagon.

"Please, sir! Please don't make us get rid of them!" I cried.

"Get rid of them?" asked the captain.

"Please!" I pleaded.

"You've got a fortune there in that wagon," said Captain Jonah.

"I don't understand, sir," I said.

"Cats are rare as hen's teeth in Oregon," explained the captain. "Folks think of the darnedest things to bring. But nobody remembers to bring cats along. Oregon's overrun with mice and mighty short on cats."

I was so mixed up, I couldn't quite understand what Captain Jonah was saying. But somehow I knew it was all right to have Snuggs and the kittens.

"My wife would sure prize one of them kittens," said the captain.

I managed to say, "There's still two not promised. Take your pick."

"Thank you," said the captain. "I'll leave the picking to Mrs. Jonah."

Then he rode off and left us to tend the broken wheel.

Rosie dashed back to our wagon. "Kate," she cried, "it's tough beans for me leaving you behind. But I can't abandon Pa. Shoot, why am I carrying on like this? You'll catch up tomorrow."

Big Rosie, who could take care of everybody, had a tear running down her cheek. I watched her rush back to her wagon. I felt like crying myself. It was just like leaving Doris in Jackson. Except now my friend was leaving me. And it was scary seeing all the wagons go.

By the time Pa fixed the wheel, it was dark.

"Hurry! We've got miles to make up," he said. And he pushed the horses as fast as he dared.

"Pray for a bright moon," said Pa. "Driving by night is the only way we're going to catch up."

But low-hanging clouds blocked out the moon and the stars. It started to rain. "We'll have to stop," said Pa. "It's foolhardy to go on."

"Might as well try to get some sleep," Ma said.

It was warm under the quilts. I dozed and dreamed—bad dreams about Rosie and me being lost in the dark mountains.

I woke with a start. Snuggs was walking on the quilt that covered me.

"What's the matter, mommy cat?" I asked.

Then I realized it wasn't raining. A bright patch of moonlight cut through the back of the wagon. The kittens were playing with one another in the silver moonlight.

"Snuggs," I whispered, "you're one smart cat, waking me up. The moon's out! It's so bright you can see everything!"

"Pa! Pa!" I called. "Wake up! The rain's stopped. We can get moving!"

Pa jumped up.

"By golly, our luck's changed. We'll catch up now!" he cried.

Day was breaking when we saw the wagon train camp on the crest of the mountains.

When we pulled into camp, Rosie ran to meet our wagon.

"I knew you'd make it!" she shouted. "I've got breakfast ready."

While we were eating, Snuggs hopped from the wagon and joined us.

"All right, you little beggar," said Rosie. "Here's a piece of bacon for you."

The sun suddenly popped out, round and red and beautiful.

Captain Jonah's big voice boomed, "Look, folks. There it is. That's Oregon down there!"

From our high perch you could see miles of wild, beautiful valleys stretching before us. For a moment no one said anything.

Then Duffy let out a yell and turned a cartwheel.

Pa put his arm around Ma. "Now, that looks like a place where we can really settle down."

Rosie came over and stood beside me.

"Looks like a choice bowl of beans to me," she said. "What do you think?"

I patted Snuggs and said, "Real choice beans."

About the Author

WILLIAM H. HOOKS was born and raised on a farm in North Carolina, where his great-grandmother told him many stories about relatives who had pulled up stakes and headed west in horse-drawn wagons. These stories were part of his inspiration for writing *Pioneer Cat*.

William H. Hooks lives in New York City with three generations of cats; the oldest one is named Snuggs. He has written dozens of books for young readers.

About the Illustrator

CHARLES ROBINSON has illustrated many children's books, including *The Ghost in Tent 19,* by Jim and Jane O'Connor, and several of Robert Newton Peck's Soup books. "I had a lot of fun illustrating *Pioneer Cat* because that era has always been fascinating to me," he says. "I never traveled in a covered wagon, but it sure must have been some experience."

Charles Robinson lives with his wife in Mendham, New Jersey.